P9-EDG-120

Peter and Lotta's Adventure

A story told and illustrated by

Elsa Beskow

Floris Books

First published in Swedish under the title
Petter och Lotta på äventyr by Albert Bonniers, Stockholm in 1929
First published in English in 2003 by Floris Books
15 Harrison Gardens, Edinburgh

1

British Library CIP data available
ISBN 0-86315-398-4 Printed in Belgium

You have probably heard the story of Aunt Green, Aunt Brown, and Aunt Lavender? If so, you are bound to remember that they had a cat called Esmerelda.

One day Esmerelda had three sweet little kittens. The white one was called Snowball, the black one Purr, and the little grey one Misty. It was Peter and Lotta who hit upon the names, and little Dot helped by waving his tail when he approved of their suggestions.

They were all delighted with the new kittens. But Aunt Green said she had such trouble teaching Esmerelda to leave the birds in the garden alone that she did not wish to keep more than one kitten. Peter and Lotta chose to keep little Snowball.

Peter and Lotta were allowed to give away Purr and Misty. They went immediately to Uncle Blue to give him his choice of the kittens, but Uncle Blue did not want to have a cat at all. Then they took the kittens out to Beata in the kitchen and she was so delighted with little Misty that she wanted to have her. But to whom they were going to give little Purr, the children had no idea.

The next day Uncle Blue was talking to the children about how to be really good, and told them that sometimes one can make nasty people good, just by being really kind to them. Peter and Lotta remembered that Washerwoman Wendy, in whose house they had lived before they came to the aunts, had been quite nasty to them sometimes. Then Lotta had the idea of giving little Purr to Wendy because that might make Wendy very, very good. Peter thought that was a good idea, but said they should not mention it to anyone because one should not go around telling people when one has done a good deed.

EB.

Early next morning, Uncle Blue came and fetched the aunts in a carriage to take them to the market. Peter and Lotta were not allowed to go, for Uncle Blue said they were too small. Nor was little Dot allowed to go; he was shut in Aunt Brown's room.

The aunts gave the children a bagful of buns and cakes and Uncle Blue said they were to be very good. And the aunts said the same thing before they waved goodbye.

Peter and Lotta had just been talking about how to be really good, and now when the aunts also told them to be good, they decided to go to Wendy with little Purr. They took the bag with the buns and cakes along because they knew that Wendy was very fond of sweet things.

But little Dot, who was in Aunt Brown's room, became quite wild when he saw through the window Peter and Lotta going away. For a whole hour he carried on barking, until Beata came to fetch some cinnamon from Aunt Brown's spice shelf. Then little Dot dashed out of the door and made off in the same direction as the children.

When Peter and Lotta arrived at Wendy's gate, they noticed that Wendy was down by the brook washing laundry, so they slipped in through the gate and put the bag with the cakes and the basket with Purr on the doorstep. Then they hid in the lilac bushes to see how Wendy would behave when she saw Purr.

After a while, Wendy heard a mewing from the basket so she went over and lifted the lid. And Peter and Lotta saw her pick up little Purr and caress him, and she said in such a gentle voice, "What a little darling!" And she fetched a saucer of cream and gave it to Purr to drink.

That made Peter and Lotta so happy and they started to slip away quietly because they knew now that Wendy would be kind to little Purr.

But at that very moment, little Dot came rushing into the garden and barked at them. When Wendy saw Peter and Lotta hiding, she got very angry and asked them what mischief they were up to.

Then little Dot started barking at Wendy and tugged at her skirt so she had to jump up on a bench. Peter had quite a job to calm little Dot down.

Lotta told Wendy they had only come to give her the cakes and little Purr as a present. Wendy said it was very good of them, and if they would just wait while she hung up the laundry, she would make waffles for them. But Peter and Lotta said they would hang up the laundry while she made the waffles.

Wendy made them so many waffles and was so kind that Peter and Lotta really understood how right Uncle Blue had been about making nasty people good.

When the time came to wave goodbye at the gate, the children were extremely happy with how their good deed had turned out.

At that moment a farmer was driving past to the mill with a load of sacks of rye, and he asked the children if they wanted a ride. Peter and Lotta agreed because it was hot and they had a long way to go. They sat down among the sacks. Dot curled up and fell asleep and in a moment the children, too, were asleep. Meanwhile the farmer, deep in thought, completely forgot about his passengers at the back of the cart.

EB

Peter and Lotta did not wake up until the cart stopped at the mill, and were startled to see how far they had travelled. The farmer said the best thing was for them to stay there until he had got the grain ground because then he would give them a lift home.

Peter and Lotta stood looking at the miller's children, and little Dot looked at the miller's little pup, and nobody dared say anything. But all of a sudden the pup said "Woof!" and put its head on one side and looked so funny that all the children had to laugh. Right away the pup and little Dot were best friends. And the children, too, played together.

After a while, Peter and Lotta realized that Beata must be worrying about them being away so long, so they went to ask the farmer about going home soon. But he sat smoking a pipe and chatting with the miller — they had not even started to grind yet.

Peter and Lotta thought that they had better walk home. The miller's wife said to take the road through the wood, but to remember to take the right and not the left when the road branched. Peter and Lotta strode off, but they could not get little Dot to come no matter how much they called. He was watching a hedgehog and neither heard nor saw anything else. The children thought he would catch up with them. He was very clever at finding his way.

EB

When Peter and Lotta reached the place in the wood where the road branched, they had to think. They were not quite sure which way to go although Uncle Blue had taken so much trouble teaching them left from right.

As they stood there, a chimney-sweep came along. Peter knew that chimney-sweeps are not dangerous, so he asked him which was right and which was left. And the chimney-sweep laughed so that his white teeth shone and held his arms out. "This is left, and this is right," the chimney-sweep said. "Are you such babies that you don't know that?"

"You see, I was right," said Lotta when the chimney-sweep had gone. And so Peter and Lotta started along the wrong road, because neither of them took into account that the chimney-sweep had been facing them so that his right was their left. You see how silly it is not to learn right and left properly!

Walking through the wood, they came to a brook and decided to take a dip. While they were playing in the water, they heard footsteps, and when they peeped out, they saw an old woman with a black kerchief on her head and a sack on her back. They hid, thinking that perhaps she was a witch. The old woman stopped when she saw the children's clothes lying beside the brook.

"Is anybody there?" she called, but Peter and Lotta did not dare answer.

So the old woman took the clothes and put them in her sack and went on, because she thought it was a pity to leave the clothes in the wood to get ruined. When the old woman had gone, Peter and Lotta crept out of the bushes, but they had no clothes to put on, and a cloud now covered the sun so it was not warm any longer but actually quite chilly.

There they stood, naked, in the middle of the wild wood and did not know what to do. They were so unhappy they started to cry. Just then an old woodcutter came walking along the path, and he comforted them and told them they could come along with him to his cottage. Perhaps his wife would have some clothes for them. So they went along with him.

The woodcutter's wife was very kind, and she immediately picked clothes out of the clothes chest and dressed Peter and Lotta in them. And when the woodcutter and his wife heard where Peter and Lotta lived, they shook their heads and said that it was more than twelve miles to get there.

That made Peter and Lotta very upset, but the old man said they could go with him to the fair for he was going to take a calf there. There was sure to be someone at the fair to give them a ride home in the evening, the old man said.

The old woman put a kerchief on Lotta and tied it under her chin, and put a hat on Peter's head. The children thought this was fine because now perhaps Uncle Blue would not recognize them. As he had said they were too small to go to the fair, he would be annoyed if he caught sight of them.

When Peter and Lotta arrived at the fair, they saw a big merry-go-round. Next to the merry-go-round there was a huge circus tent. Peter and Lotta stopped at this tent while the kind woodcutter went off to sell his calf. He promised the children he would find somebody to take them home.

Suddenly the children saw Uncle Blue and the aunts having a ride on the merry-go-round, and they hurried away to hide. A funny man dressed as a clown was standing by the door of the tent, and when he caught sight of Peter and Lotta he shouted, "Well now, Granny and Grandpa, I bid you welcome!" And he pulled them into the tent.

Inside, there was a man who swallowed swords and ate fire, and another who walked on a tightrope. Then a tame bear appeared stepping in time to the music, and the clown lifted Peter and Lotta up on its back, though Lotta struggled, and the bear padded around with them, and the clown shouted, "Houp-la, little Granny and Grandpa!" Peter thought it was fun having a ride on a live bear. But at that moment, just when the people were clapping, Uncle Blue and the aunts came in. Aunt Lavender cried out and fainted, and Uncle Blue rushed up and snatched the children and there was a great to-do.

All this excitement made Peter and Lotta so giddy that they did not know what was going on until they were sitting in the carriage with the aunts and Uncle Blue rolling along home.

All the aunts were talking at the same time. Aunt Green asked how they had dared to go the fair without permission, and Aunt Brown said she had never thought they would be so disobedient, and Aunt Lavender asked them why on earth they had dressed up like that. And Uncle Blue said, “This time the birch switch must be used, that is quite obvious!”

The children could barely explain things, because Lotta was crying so much she could not speak, and Peter did not know how to start. Then all of a sudden little Dot came rushing towards them up the road, quite beside himself with joy at seeing them. Poor little Dot, he had been looking for the children for hours!

Aunt Brown said, “How on earth did little Dot get out of my room? Did you let him out?”

“No, he didn’t catch up with us until we were at Wendy’s place,” Peter said.

“Have you been to Wendy’s place?” Uncle Blue asked astonished. “What were you doing there?”

At last Uncle Blue and the aunts heard the whole story. And they were so sorry for the children who had been left standing there in the wood without any clothes. Uncle Blue said nothing, so Peter and Lotta wondered if the birch switch would appear when they got home. But it did not. Uncle Blue said they had been good children who had paid attention to what he taught them. But next time they intended to do a special good deed, they should ask his advice first.

Then he added that if next morning they could tell right from left when he asked them, they could come with him to the fair and have a ride on the merry-go-round.

The children were now quite sure about left and right because all they had to do was remember that right was opposite to the direction they took in the wood. On the way to the fair, they gave the borrowed clothes back to the woodcutter and his wife, who went with them to the fair, and Uncle Blue treated them to a ride on the merry-go-round, and they all had a wonderful time.

But Esmerelda and little Snowball remained at home because nowhere were they happier than at home in Aunt Brown's kitchen. They had no wish at all to go out in search of adventure in the wide world.